Disney · PIXAR

TOY STORY

BUZZ O

By Lisa Papademetriou
Illustrated by Frederico Mancuso, Giorgio Vallorani, and the Disney Storybook Artists

Random House New York

ISBN: 978-0-7364-2841-5
www.randomhouse.com/kids
MANUFACTURED IN CHINA
10 9 8 7 6 5 4 3 2 1

One afternoon, Bonnie went to the park with Woody, Jessie, and Dolly. She left Buzz Lightyear in charge of the rest of her toys.

As soon as Bonnie was gone, the Peas-in-a-Pod began bouncing on their shelf. "Let's play!" they shouted.

"Wait!" said Buzz. "This looks dangerous."

Suddenly, Slinky, the Alien toys, and the peas all fell off the shelf and landed right on top of the startled space ranger.

Buzz stood up, struck a dance pose, and snapped his fingers.
The other toys groaned. Buzz was in Spanish mode again!
"The return of Señor Space Nut," said Mr. Potato Head.

Buzz grabbed a curtain from the dollhouse and held it up like a bullfighter's cape.
"Hold on, Buzz," said Slinky. "You're not yourself."
Hamm tried to tackle Buzz, but Buzz stepped aside and the piggy bank went sliding across the floor.

CRASH! Hamm hit the bookshelf and flipped over. As the toys looked on, a book fell on its side and teetered over Buzz's head.

"Buzz, look out!" cried Rex. But it was too late—the book tumbled right on top of the space ranger!

"Buzz!" shouted Rex. "Are you okay?"

"Buzz!" repeated Buzz. "Are you okay?"

"Hey!" Rex turned to Mr. Potato Head. "That's what I just said."

"Hey!" repeated Buzz again. "That's what I just said."

Mr. Potato Head looked at Rex. "He must have gotten knocked into Repeat mode," he explained.

"What do we do?" asked Rex. The toys had to get Buzz back to normal before Bonnie came home!

"We're gonna have to jiggle his wires," said Hamm. "Let's bounce him on the bed."

The toys pulled Buzz onto Bonnie's bed.
"Jump!" yelled Hamm.
They bounced up and down, but Buzz still didn't go back to normal.
Hamm told Rex to make his biggest jump. **Boing!** Buzz bounced right off the bed . . .

. . . and landed facedown on the floor! The toys poked Buzz.
They shook him. They even tickled him. But Buzz didn't budge.
Suddenly, they heard the sound of a car door slamming. Bonnie was home!

"Hurry!" shouted Hamm. "We've got to fix Buzz!"
Rex opened Buzz's back panel and stared
nervously at a tangle of wires.
"Which one?" Rex asked. "Red or blue?"

Just then, the toys heard a noise outside
the door. They went limp as Bonnie's mom
walked in with Bonnie's backpack.

"Bonnie!" she called when she saw that
there were toys everywhere. "Please come
clean up this room!"

"It *is* clean, Mom!" Bonnie called back.

When Bonnie's mom left, Woody, Jessie, and Dolly jumped out of the backpack.
Jessie spotted Buzz on the floor.

"Buzz, are you okay?" she asked.

"It's not my fault!" cried Rex. "There are too many wires!"

Jessie pulled Buzz up and whacked him on the back.

Everyone was silent. Suddenly, Buzz blinked and looked from side to side.

"Do I have something on my face?" he asked. "Why is everyone staring?"

The toys cheered with relief. Buzz was back to normal!

"All right, everyone!" called Woody. "Let's clean this room before Bonnie comes back!"

The toys finished tidying up just as Bonnie walked in.

"Thanks for looking after everyone, Buzz," Bonnie said. "I knew this place would be okay with you in charge!"

SHOWTIME!

By Christine Peymani
Illustrated by Mario Cortés and Mike Inman

Random House New York

ISBN: 978-0-7364-2841-5
www.randomhouse.com/kids
MANUFACTURED IN CHINA
10 9 8 7 6 5 4 3 2 1

One afternoon while Bonnie was out, her toys decided to put on a talent show. Everyone was very excited as they began to build sets, choose costumes, and practice their routines.

But Buzz Lightyear didn't know what to do. He had many talents, but he wanted to pick the very best one—the one that would impress Jessie the cowgirl the most.

When Buzz saw Hamm and Buttercup practicing their comedy act, he decided to join them.

"I can do impressions!" said Buzz. He put on Woody's hat. "Howdy, partners. I'm Sheriff Woody. Did you know there's a snake in my boot?"

"Since when does Woody sound like that?" asked Hamm. Buttercup chuckled.

Just then, Buzz noticed that Mr. Pricklepants and the Aliens were practicing a play.
"We're doing a classic: *Romeo and Juliet*!" said Mr. Pricklepants.
"Great!" said Buzz. "But don't you think the play would be much better if we changed it to *Romeo and Juliet . . . in Space*?"
"I don't think so . . . ," replied Mr. Pricklepants.

Rex and Trixie were acting out scenes from their favorite
Buzz Lightyear video game for Jessie.
"I just feel like something is missing," said Rex with a frown.
"Maybe that something is *me*!" declared Buzz.

Buzz demonstrated his best space ranger moves. "To infinity . . . and beyond!" he shouted when he was done.

Rex and Trixie looked at each other. "That's not what happens in the game," Rex whispered to Trixie.

Suddenly, Buzz heard Slinky calling him. "Hey, Buzz! Take a look at that fancy footwork!" Buzz turned to see Woody and Bullseye practicing their rodeo tricks. But a rodeo didn't eed a space ranger. Buzz still didn't know what his act should be!

"Time to start the show!" called Dolly.

"Are you ready, Buzz?" asked Jessie. "I can't wait to see your act!"

Buzz smiled nervously. He didn't *have* an act!

The toys gathered around the stage, and Bullseye turned on the radio.

As music filled the room, Buzz's body began to shake. His arm started to twitch. Then his foot started to move.

The other toys stared in amazement as Buzz began to dance. He danced across the room to Jessie. Then he grabbed her, dipped her, and gave her a twirl.

"Uh, I don't know why I did that," said Buzz, blushing.

But Jessie knew exactly what had happened—the music had switched Buzz to Spanish mode!

"It's okay, Buzz," whispered Jessie. "Just go with it!"

"Well then," said Buzz. "May I have this dance?"
Jessie nodded, and the two began to spin, twirl, dip, and whirl across the stage.
The other toys clapped and cheered. Buzz's act was a hit!

When the music ended, Buzz and Jessie took a bow.
Buzz was thrilled! He had discovered a hidden talent and impressed
Jessie at the same time. What a perfect way to kick off the talent show!